# A Pickle
# for a Nickel

*A Golden Read-it-yourself Book*

*By* LILIAN MOORE

*Illustrated by*
SUSAN PERL

GOLDEN PRESS

NEW YORK

Library of Congress Catalog Card Number: 61-12364

© Copyright 1961 by Golden Press, Inc. All rights reserved, including the right of reproduction in whole or in part in any form. Designed and produced by Artists and Writers Press, Inc. Printed in the U.S.A. by Western Printing and Lithographing Company. Published by Golden Press, Inc., New York. Published simultaneously in Canada by The Musson Book Company, Ltd., Toronto.

Mr. Benjamin Bumble lived
by himself in an old brown house
on Round-About Road.

Well, he did not really live there
all by himself.

He had a parrot.

Mr. Bumble liked his parrot very much.

But you will not guess why!

He liked his parrot
because it did not talk.

Mr. Benjamin Bumble was a quiet man.

He liked everything around him
to be quiet, too.

His clock did not go
**TICK-TOCK TICK-TOCK.**
It went tick-tick-tick.

His doorbell did not go
**RING-DING-DING.**
It went ping.

And his parrot did not talk.

"That's my good Pedro,"
Mr. Bumble told his parrot.
"That's my good quiet Pedro!"

Every morning Mr. Bumble went off
to work in his car.

His car did not go
CHUG-CHUG-CHUG.
It went purr-rr-r.

Every evening Mr. Bumble came home
to his quiet house and
his quiet parrot Pedro.

And Mr. Bumble was happy.

Down the road
not far from Mr. Bumble
there was a little white house.
For a long time no one lived there.

Then one day some people came
to live in the little white house.

"Hm," said Mr. Bumble,
"I see a man.

"Hm," said Mr. Bumble,
"I see a woman.

"Oh, dear," said Mr. Bumble,
"I see a BOY!
Boys like firecrackers!
Boys play cowboys and Indians!
Boys like NOISE!"

Mr. Bumble did not meet the boy.

Every morning he went off
to work in his quiet little car.
So there were things Mr. Bumble
did not know.

He did not know that the boy
was William.

He did not know that William
was lonely.

He did not know that William
came up Round-About Road
to see who lived in the old brown house.

Mr. Bumble did not meet William.
But Pedro did.

The parrot sat in his cage at the
open window, looking out
at the world.

"Hello!" said William.

The parrot said nothing.

"Do you want a pickle for a nickel?"
asked William.

The parrot said nothing.

He put his head to one side and
looked at the boy.

After that, William could not
keep away from the parrot.

Every day he came up
Round-About Road to the
old brown house.

Mr. Bumble never did see him.
But Pedro did—every day.

William talked and talked
to the parrot.

He said all kinds of funny things
to Pedro.

But Pedro just looked at William
and did not say a word.

One evening Mr. Bumble came home
from work in his
quiet little car,
and went into his quiet house.

All at once there was a loud cry,
"Want a pickle for a nickel?"

Mr. Bumble jumped back.

Who was in his house?

There was another scream.

"Pickle! Pickle! Pickle!
For a nickel!"

Mr. Bumble ran into the living room.
It was Pedro, screaming in his cage.

Quickly, Mr. Bumble put
the cover over Pedro's cage.

Now Pedro was quiet again,
but poor Mr. Bumble!

He was so upset
he could not eat his supper.

"Dear me," thought Mr. Bumble.
"I hope he is better in the morning."

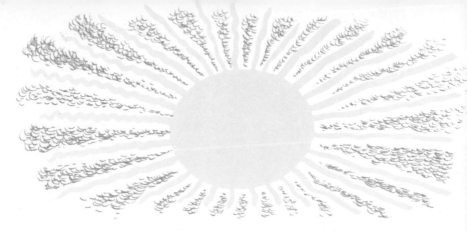

But in the morning, Pedro screamed,
"Jack and Jill went up the hill
to get a pickle for a nickel!"

And in the evening Pedro screamed,
"Yankee Doodle went to town.
Macaroni! Get the macaroni!"

After that there was no more quiet
for Mr. Bumble.

He did not know what to do.

Then one morning Mr. Bumble
looked out the window.

He looked at the little white house,
and saw the boy sitting outside
all by himself.

"Firecrackers!

Cowboys and Indians!
Boys like NOISE!" said Mr. Bumble.

Mr. Bumble took the cage with Pedro in it.

Then he walked down Round-About Road
just as fast as he could.
He walked right up
to the little white house.
He walked right up to William.

"Boy," said Mr. Bumble,
"Do you want a parrot?"

William looked at Pedro.
He looked at Mr. Bumble.

"A parrot!" cried William.
"For me?"

"I do not want this parrot any more,"
said Mr. Bumble.

"Are you sure?" asked William.
He could not believe it was true.
"Are you sure?"

"Oh yes, oh yes," said Mr. Bumble.
"I am sure!
Pedro talks too much.
He was a nice quiet bird.
Now he talks and talks.
I don't know what's happened to him.
Do you want him?"

William wanted to say,
"Oh yes! Yes, I do!"

But first he had to do something.

He ran into the house.

He ran right out again
because his mother said . . . yes,
he could have the parrot.

"Come, come!" said Mr. Bumble.
"Do you want the parrot?"

William wanted to say, "Yes! Yes! Yes!"

But first he had to say something.
Maybe Mr. Bumble would not give him
the parrot after all.
But William had to say it.

"Mr. Bumble," said William,
"I didn't know you wanted a quiet parrot.
I . . . I . . . I . . . was the one
who made him talk!"

"You!" said Mr. Bumble.

He put Pedro's cage down.

"Well, then," he said.

"You made him talk.

Now you will have to keep him.

Good day!"

And Mr. Bumble walked away
as fast as he could—
away from the little white house,
and up Round-About Road.

William ran to the cage and
took off the cover.

"Oh, Pedro!" he said to the bird.
"Now you're my parrot!"

"Want a pickle for a nickel?"
asked Pedro.

Mr. Bumble did not hear him.

Mr. Bumble was back in his house,
his quiet little house
where the clock went tick and
the doorbell went ping.

Mr. Bumble was happy again.